THE BUTTERFLY SECRET

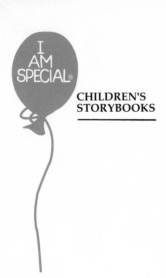

CHILDREN'S
STORYBOOKS

THE BUTTERFLY SECRET

Published by
OUR SUNDAY VISITOR PUBLISHING
200 Noll Plaza
Huntington, Indiana 46750

Original text first published in the 2nd Edition Teacher Guide of the
I AM SPECIAL® Kindergarten Program.

I AM SPECIAL® is a registered trademark of
Our Sunday Visitor Publishing
Our Sunday Visitor, Inc.

Early Childhood Consultant: Joan Ensor Plum
Project Director: Paul S. Plum
Typesetting and Mechanicals: Fugger & Fugger Graphic Communications

ISBN: 0-87973-017-X (hardcover)
ISBN: 0-87973-014-5 (softcover)
Printed in the U.S.A.

THE BUTTERFLY SECRET

By Carol Therese Plum   Illustrated by Andee Most

One bright spring day, a tiny yellow caterpillar crawled out of his egg and onto the leaf of an apple tree. All around him, lovely white apple blossoms nodded in welcome, stirred by a gentle breeze.

"What a wonderful place I have come to!"
thought the little caterpillar, nibbling happily on his juicy green leaf.

As the days passed, it seemed that the little caterpillar was always hungry. He grew

BIGGER

and

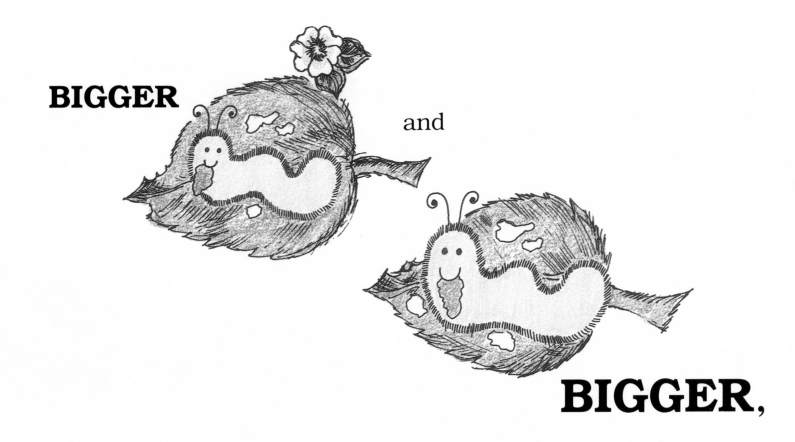

BIGGER,

and he was perfectly content to munch on leaves and nod at the apple blossoms.

A day came, however, when the caterpillar became bored with eating. The lovely white petals had fallen to the ground, and he had already explored all the branches of his tree. Summer had come, and it was time to see the world.

Crawling down from
his branch, the caterpillar felt
very excited and also a little scared. How tall
and frightening the orchard looked from the ground!

"Goodbye!"

he called to his dear apple tree as he wiggled on his way.

During his journey, the caterpillar saw many strange and wonderful things. He found delicious plants to eat and friendly creatures to visit.

In the daytime,
the summer sun shined warmly on his fuzzy yellow back.

At night, a silvery moon lighted his way from a sky of stars that merrily winked at him.

One day the caterpillar came to the edge of the orchard. Beyond the last row of trees, he found a wide, sunny meadow and an endless stretch of blue sky above it.

There the caterpillar saw the most beautiful creatures he had ever seen.
They flew above the meadow on fragile wings of rainbow colors
and drank sweet nectar from the wildflowers below.
The caterpillar had heard of such creatures
on his journey through the orchard.
They were butterflies.

"Hello!"

he called to them. But the lovely butterflies
were too busy and too far away to notice him.

Day after day, the caterpillar crawled to the edge of the orchard to watch the butterflies. He was enchanted by their delicate, fluttering wings, yet he also felt sad and sorry for himself.

"They are such beautiful creatures," thought the lonely caterpillar, "and I am just a fuzzy worm. They can fly high above the meadow, but I must crawl on the ground."

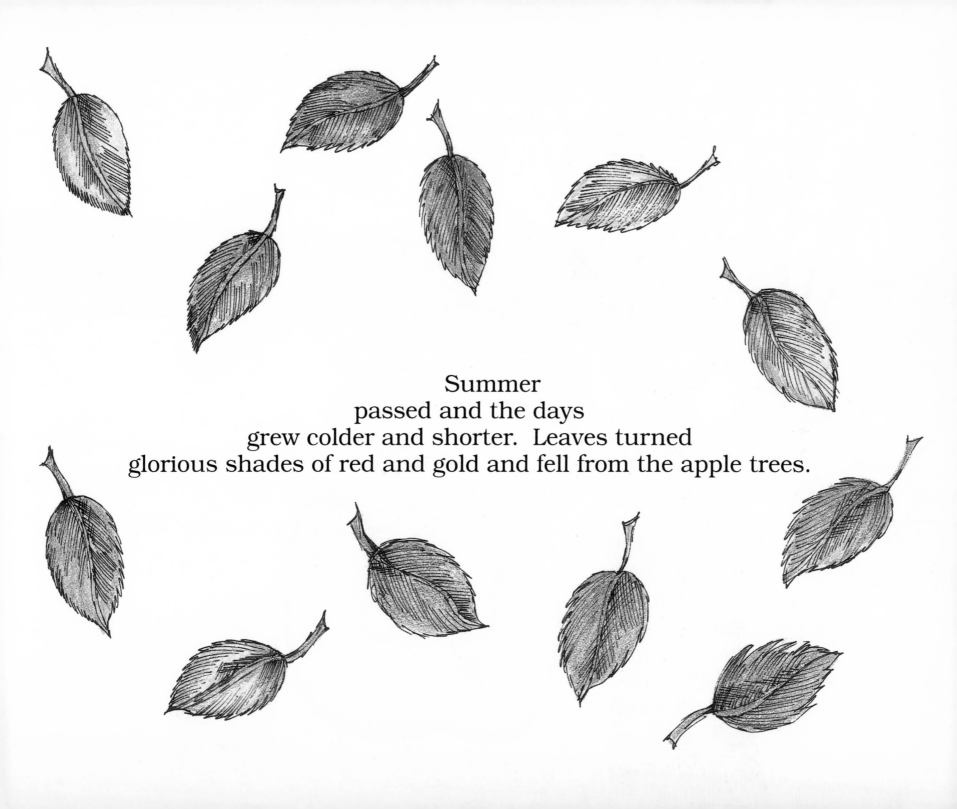

Summer
passed and the days
grew colder and shorter. Leaves turned
glorious shades of red and gold and fell from the apple trees.

One morning, the caterpillar
awoke to find the orchard
floor covered with cold
white frost.

When he went to watch the butterflies, he was shocked to see that for the first time they were not flying about the meadow!

Now the caterpillar felt miserable.

Where had all the butterflies gone? He climbed to a strong branch in his new tree and spun a thick cocoon to keep him warm when cold winter winds would blow.

Then he cried himself to sleep.

Many months later, gentle breezes again stirred white apple blossoms on the orchard trees. Sensing that the winter days had fled, the caterpillar awoke and crawled out of his cocoon.

Somehow he felt very different . . .

The caterpillar's fuzzy yellow body was replaced by fragile wings of rainbow colors that were drying in the sun.

"What magic is this?" exclaimed the beautiful creature. "Why, I have become a butterfly!"

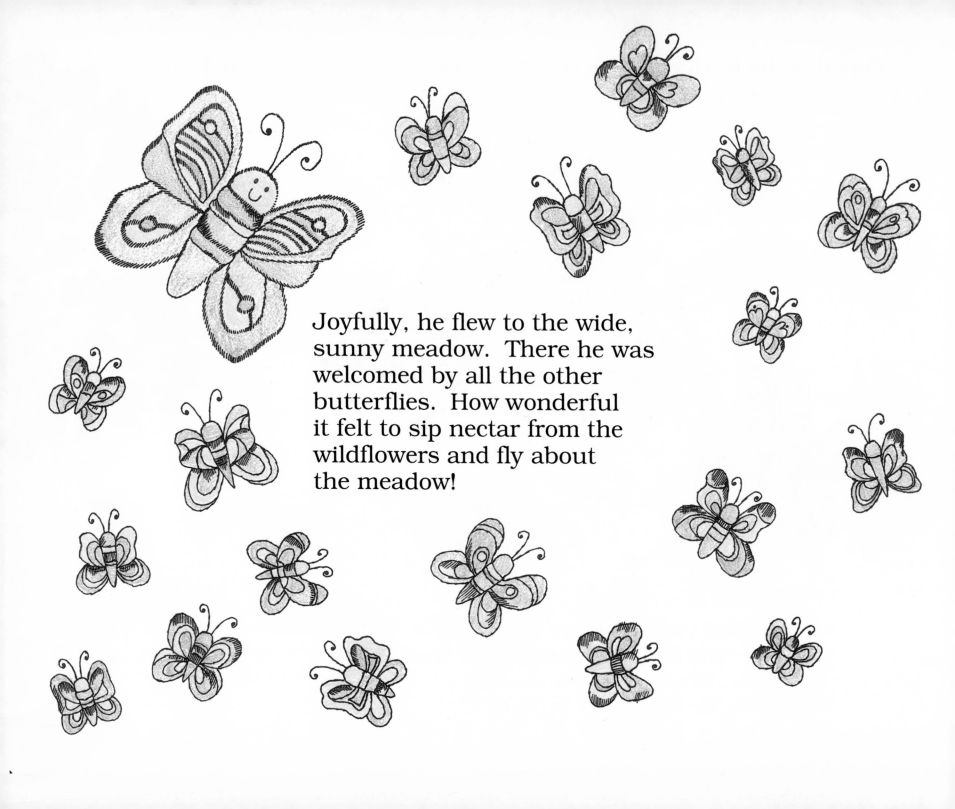

Joyfully, he flew to the wide, sunny meadow. There he was welcomed by all the other butterflies. How wonderful it felt to sip nectar from the wildflowers and fly about the meadow!

One day the butterfly noticed a fuzzy yellow caterpillar watching him from the edge of the orchard.

"Shall I tell him
        the butterfly secret?" he wondered.

"No," he decided. "I will let him discover it himself."